Prologue

Bulk was on his way from Mission Control to the Assembly Tower when he spotted Furno. The rookie was sitting in the records room, scrolling through some of the thousands of holographic files stored there.

"Hey, Furno," Bulk said, sticking his head in the door. "Looking for anything special? Or just taking a break from catching all those escaped criminals?"

Furno looked over his shoulder at his friend. "Well, I started out trying to find more information on some of the criminals who broke out of Hero Factory. I thought it might help me to recapture some of them if I knew more about their records."

"And?"

"One really old file is blocked," Furno answered, turning back to the screen. "It's marked classified. But it's referenced under Black Phantom, Splitface, Jawblade, Toxic Reapa, Voltix, Speeda Demon, and XT4. Seems like it would be a worthwhile record to see."

Bulk walked up to the console. "What's the file number?"

"14Y-YX6."

A smile flashed across Bulk's face. "Oh yeah — they wouldn't want you to see that one."

"Why not?"

"That, rookie, was one of Hero Factory's first big cases. . . . Let's just say it didn't go quite as we planned. There are parts of it that everybody would like to forget, even Mr. Makuro, our founder."

Furno leaned forward in his chair. "Now you've got me interested."

Bulk looked around and saw that no one was

SECRET
MISSION #2:

LEGION OF DARKNESS

BY GREG FARSHTEY

SCHOLASTIC INC.

No part of this publication may be reproduced, stored in a retrieval system, or transmitted in any form or by any means, electronic, mechanical, photocopying, recording, or otherwise, without written permission of the publisher. For information regarding permission, write to Scholastic Inc., Attention: Permissions Department, 557 Broadway, New York, NY 10012.

ISBN 978-0-545-46517-5

LEGO, the LEGO logo, and the Brick and Knob configurations are trademarks of the LEGO Group. © 2012 The LEGO Group. Produced by Scholastic Inc. under license from the LEGO Group.

Published by Scholastic Inc. SCHOLASTIC and associated logos are trademarks and/or registered trademarks of Scholastic Inc.

12 11 10 9 8 7 6 5 4 3 2   12 13 14 15 16 17/0

Printed in the U.S.A.   40

First printing, October 2012

about. Then he clapped a big hand on Furno's shoulder. "Well, what the heck . . . I don't mind telling a story on myself. Been a long time since I even thought about that case. I've got clearance, so I can call up the file for you. But you have to promise me one thing."

"What?"

"Don't tell anyone who set this up for you. There's a reason it's a secret file. There's a reason no one talks about . . . the Legion of Darkness."

1

about. The car stopped outside an old... ...her left with the... ...helping a way on in... ...you to inspect from that the... ...to... ...till roll up the... I'm... ...remind us of anything." "What..." "Don't tell anyone about this for you. The car... ...as our... ...

From the Secret Files of Hero Factory . . .

Epsilon Gamma IV

any years ago, in the early days of Hero Factory . . .

Unlike most places, night doesn't fall little by little on the fourth planet of the Epsilon Gamma system. There's no soft gray twilight and dark blue early evening there, just daylight to pitch darkness as if someone had thrown a switch. Occupants of the world make a point of finishing their business and retreating to their homes before it gets dark. This limits the amount of commerce conducted on the planet, but also saves a lot on streetlights.

Of course, any robot with good enough optic sensors can navigate in complete darkness. There are three ways to get those kinds of upgrades: pay for them, barter for them, or steal them. The two robots running down the backstreet on this particular night had opted for choice number three. That gave them the benefit of getting a good look at who was chasing them, even if they had no idea who the white-armored robot with the big blaster was or why he was pursuing.

"I thought you said you owned this town," snarled Voltix.

"I do!" Splitface replied. "I put the right bribes into the right hands, and the ones who matter look the other way when I need to 'borrow' something."

"Then who's the tin bloodhound on our trail?" asked Voltix. "We no sooner crack that safe than he's all over us. Did you cheat somebody or something? Maybe they're looking for payback?"

"Cheat him?" replied Splitface, looking back at the robot on their trail. "I wouldn't even play with him."

"How far away is the ship?"

"Too far."

"Think he's going to give up?"

"Do you?"

Voltix abruptly stopped running. "Then we fight. There are two of us and only one of him."

"That we know of," Splitface pointed out. The criminal was known for having more than one personality in his computer brain, but when things went bad, the more cautious one took control. This could make him a very annoying partner to have, especially when he insisted that both sides of him needed a separate cut of the loot.

"You're getting soft, Splitface," said Voltix. "Been too long since you've had to blast your way off a planet."

Splitface turned to face his sometime partner. "Right, like you've had to make so many daring escapes. When's the last time anyone tried to stop a crime? Local security on most of these worlds is a joke—they only use robots that aren't good enough to be turned into household appliances."

"Quiet, he's coming," hissed Voltix. "I'll fry him, and you do . . . whatever it is you do these days."

The robot in the white armor had been following the two criminals by bounding across rooftops. Now he paused at the edge of the nearest building, scanning for his targets. He saw no sign of them. His tracking computer had calculated their average speed as well as the map of the area and indicated that they could not have lost him on foot. An instant sensor scan revealed no traces of teleportation or any type of vehicle exhaust.

That meant they were still down there, just hiding. He loved it when they tried to hide.

"Attention," he said. "My name is Preston Stormer. Power down your weapons and surrender. You are under arrest in the name of Hero Factory."

The point of an ambush is to stay quiet so

your prey doesn't know you are waiting. But at the mention of "Hero Factory," Splitface couldn't keep silent.

"Hero what?" he said. "What's a Hero Factory? Is that someplace they train crazy robots who want to get a pounding?"

"Ask him when he's on the ground," snapped Voltix, unleashing two electrical blasts at Stormer. The bright flashes illuminated the dark city for miles around.

Expecting the attack, the robot called Stormer narrowly dodged the bolts and responded with a force blast of his own. It missed Voltix, on purpose, but drove the villain back to cover. Stormer wasn't out to kill these criminals. That wasn't what Hero Factory was going to be about.

"You want him down?" growled Splitface. "I'll bring him down."

With that, he slammed a heavily armored fist into the side of the building. The resulting tremor made Stormer lose his footing. He fell, grabbing on to ledges and banner poles on the way down to slow his descent. He still hit hard, and it cost him precious seconds as his hardware systems readjusted to compensate.

In that time, Splitface and Voltix closed in. Both were smiling. "He doesn't look so tough," said Splitface. "Pretty armor, though. Gonna be a shame to dirty it up."

"Maybe he's a factory reject." Voltix chuckled. "Hey, Stormer, maybe we should send you back to the manufacturing building in pieces. Maybe they'll build you right the next time."

Stormer got to his feet. "Laugh if you like. You and your kind have done a lot of that over the years. But even if I don't stop you, some other Hero will. Hero Factory is everywhere, and your days are numbered."

"That's funny," said Voltix. "I could say the same about you."

Just as the villain was about to unleash his lightning, something struck him in the center of his back. While he felt the impact, it wasn't enough to knock him down. But he could tell that whatever had hit him was stuck to his back, and even more ominous, it was making a beeping noise that sounded suspiciously like a countdown.

"What is that? Get it off!" Voltix said to Splitface.

Splitface peered at Voltix's back and then took several quick steps away. "It looks like a metal ball, and there's a screen on it with a clock showing seconds ticking down. Somebody doesn't like you very much, Voltix."

"That's one way to put it."

The new voice belonged to a green-armored robot carrying two projectile launchers. He was standing behind the two villains.

"You just got introduced to the latest from the Hero Factory weapons labs—a magnetic mine. Once it attaches, only a Hero knows the code to remove it. I'd say you have about thirty seconds, Voltix, to make me so pleased with you that I turn it off."

"Splitface!" Voltix cried. "Do something, you—"

Voltix's partner did indeed do something. He ran off, surprisingly fast for someone so big. Stormer gave chase but had to return a few moments later empty-handed.

"He got away," said Stormer.

"So I see." The green robot was tying a length of chain around Voltix's wrists. Stormer noted that the chain wasn't metal, but made of a plastic that wouldn't conduct electricity. "We got this one, anyway."

"Did you enter the code, Thresher?" Stormer asked.

The green robot smiled. "What code, rookie?"

"The magnetic mine—"

Thresher laughed. "Well, it is magnetic, and it does belong to me, so it's mine. But that's about it. There's no code, and nothing happens when the countdown ends—except that it starts again."

"What?" exclaimed Stormer.

"What?!" yelled Voltix.

Thresher leaned in close to Voltix. "We don't blow folks up. That's one of the things that makes us different from you. I could list the others, but we would be here all night. Stormer, get the Hero craft and let's get this crook to jail."

Later, piloting his Hero craft through the darkness of space, Stormer found he couldn't contain his curiosity. "So, Thresher, how would you rate my performance?"

Thresher thought for a moment and then said, "You did very well. It's just too bad you're dead." Seeing Stormer's surprised look, he added, "Think about it. If I hadn't shown up as backup, Voltix and Splitface would have made this your last mission."

The Alpha Team leader began to tick off items on the fingers of his right hand as he maneuvered the ship through an asteroid field. "One, you let yourself be spotted way too early in your pursuit; two, you obviously didn't study the files or you would have known what Splitface was capable of; and three, I need smart, quick, and very much *alive* Heroes on my team. Dead ones I can find all over. The ability to make a noble speech just before the bad guys wipe you out doesn't make you any the less destroyed, Stormer."

The white-armored hero nodded. Thresher was right, of course. He had made one of the worst mistakes a Hero could make: He had assumed the battle was over, and so he had lost. The first lesson Thresher had taught was that there was always a way to win—it might not be clean, neat, obvious, or easy to do, but it was there. All you had to do was find it.

Someday, thought Stormer, *when I am leading rookies, I will make sure they know that. But that's a long way off.*

Bulk walked into the meeting room, pausing in the doorway to look around. It was a stark, bare room with bright white lighting overhead. One other robot was already there, a tall one with gray armor. Bulk sat down next to him and extended a hand.

"Hi, my name's Bulk," said the broad-shouldered robot. "Three guesses why."

The gray-armored robot smiled as he shook his hand. "Von Ness. Any idea what this is all about?"

Bulk shook his head. "I just got out of the Assembly Tower an hour ago. But considering all the weapons they gave us, I doubt we're going to be tending flower beds."

Von Ness chuckled. "Not unless the weeds around here have rocket launchers."

Another robot, this one with black armor, came in. He sat a few seats away from Bulk and Von Ness. He was followed shortly by Stormer, who nodded to all three and busied himself setting up a holographic presentation. When this was done, he sat down in the front row.

Thresher came in a few minutes later. He gave a brief smile to the assembled robots and stood at the front of the room to address them. "For those of you who don't know me, my name is Thresher. Going around the room, we have

Stormer, Stringer, Bulk, and Von Ness here. Welcome, all of you, to Hero Factory."

Bulk and Von Ness gave each other quizzical looks. Stringer shifted in his chair, looking a little bored.

"All of you are to be members of Alpha Team, the first active Hero Factory squad," Thresher continued. "It will be our job to keep the galaxy safe from thieves, smugglers, and worse. Criminals can be found all over, on every world. If you're expecting glory, the door out is over there — this is not about personal glory. If you're expecting to become a legend, same answer — the odds are, none of us will be remembered past the day we are decommissioned."

Thresher looked at each of the new Heroes in turn. "But if you want to feel like you made a difference, this is the place for you. If you want to power down at night knowing that traders, travelers, and working robots are a little bit safer because of something you did, then you are the kind of Hero I need on my squad." He paused for a moment, then said, "Any questions?"

Stringer raised his hand. "Just one, Chief—who asked for us?"

"I don't understand, Stringer," Thresher said.

Stringer stood up. "See, I've been scanning datafiles on a lot of the worlds out there while I was waiting for this meeting. Quite a few of these planets we're supposed to be protecting are getting rich by hiding criminals, or giving them a place to stash their loot, or selling them ships and arms when they need them. They sure aren't going to want us anywhere around. So who is it that's calling for a factory that makes Heroes?"

"Can I answer that?" Stormer asked Thresher.

"Go ahead."

Stormer got to his feet and turned to Stringer. "I understand what you're saying, but you're looking at things the wrong way. Those planets you talked about—they are working with criminals because they see no other choice. The law can't protect them. The average robot can't stand up to someone like Splitface or Voltix and hope to survive intact. So they play along. These aren't the places that will turn us away. They are the places that need us the most!"

Bulk looked over his shoulder. He expected Stringer to continue the argument or make some smart remark. Whoever this Stormer was, he sure took the whole Hero thing seriously. But instead, Stringer was just smiling, not in a nasty way, but more like he admired the guts Stormer had shown in giving that answer. In that moment, Bulk decided that Stringer was okay.

Von Ness raised his hand. "What are the odds, Thresher? I don't mind fighting. I do mind losing."

Thresher activated the holographic projector. It displayed a miniature map of the galaxy, studded with points of red light. There seemed to be hundreds of thousands of them. "Each light you see indicates that a crime was committed in that spot sometime in the last year. So to answer your question, the odds of success are pretty low. Until Hero Factory is running full force and we have more help, it's going to be the five of us against an awful lot of bad guys."

"And we think we have a chance because . . . ?" asked Von Ness.

"We're a team," said Stormer. "They're not. The plan is simple: Hero Factory will take them on one by one and beat them all."

"That's a plan?" said Von Ness, disbelief in his voice.

"And a good one," Stormer answered, with a smile.

I know how those Heroes think. They'll take us on one at a time, and eventually, they'll take us all down," Splitface muttered to himself. "Could be, it's time to find another line of work."

He was sitting in a refueling station on one of the numerous planets that let criminals recharge for a hefty fee, and no questions asked. He was a regular here. So was the shark-faced robot swimming around and around in the big water tank next to him.

"Who's going to beat who?" said the swimmer, whose name was Jawblade.

Splitface glanced at him. He could never quite remember if Jawblade was another crook or something on the menu in this place.

"Two robots busted up my robbery," Splitface complained. "Said they were from Hero Depot . . . Hero Warehouse . . . Hero Factory . . . something like that."

Jawblade swam a few more laps, thinking about what Splitface had said. Then he asked, "How do you know?"

"What do you mean, how do I know?" snapped Splitface. "I was there, wasn't I?"

"No, I mean, how do you know there's a factory? How do you know it isn't just those two guys?"

Splitface was about to insist that of course there was a factory, when he stopped himself. How *did* he know — just because those two stiffs told him? What if they were just crooks after his haul, dressing themselves up as some kind of heroes? That wouldn't explain why they grabbed Voltix . . . unless Voltix was in on it with them. That would be just the kind of thing Voltix would do, too, the crummy . . .

"Listen, me and Toxic Reapa are doing a

job tomorrow night," said Jawblade. "I know, I know . . . me and Toxic have had our problems in the past, but there aren't too many crooks who will work with me. They're always complaining about smelling like fish for a week after. Anyway, if we run into these Hero Factory types, I'll let you know. If we don't, then maybe you're worrying about nothing, pal."

Splitface liked the idea of worrying about nothing. It was a lot better than worrying about something, right?

The next night, Toxic Reapa and Jawblade were in the largest robot-made river on Sigma Pi III. While the waters were remarkable for their warmth and the abundance of fish and plant life, neither criminal had any interest in those things. What they liked about the river was the museum that sat right on its northern shore.

"Are you sure about this?" Toxic Reapa asked. His voice, never the most pleasant, was especially grating tonight, because he hated the water.

"What am I?" asked Jawblade. "I'm a crook who looks like a shark. I do underwater crimes. I make it my business to be sure about things like this."

The plan, as Jawblade had laid it out, was very simple. The museum was hosting an exhibition of precious metals. The entrances to the building were all heavily guarded by security robots—all except for one. The huge aquarium tanks that hosted native sea life exhibits recycled their water through the river. That meant there had to be a big pipe connected to the museum, and that was how Jawblade and Toxic Reapa would get in and out.

Jawblade had to admit that this was not his first choice of partners. Oh, Toxic Reapa wasn't a bad sort, for an insane thief and "wreck-stuff-for-hire" type. But his affection for toxic waste as a weapon meant he tended to glow in the dark sometimes, not to mention leaving a very easy trail to follow if one of his tanks sprang a leak, as often happened. Jawblade had wanted to do this job with Black Phantom, but no one had seen that well-known robot-breaker in weeks.

The two thieves dove underwater, Jawblade leading the way. The water was too wet for Toxic Reapa's tastes. He comforted himself with the thought that with the proceeds from this robbery he would be able to afford much better waste tanks.

The pair ran into their first unpleasant surprise when they reached the pipe. There was an iron grille at the end, probably there to keep fish from swimming up into the aquarium from the river. Jawblade swam close, grabbed the grille in his teeth, and tore it off.

With the way open, they swam up into the pipe. It was narrow enough that they had to travel single file, which made Jawblade nervous. He didn't like someone with a toxic waste shooter being right behind him. After all, now that Toxic Reapa was in, he didn't really need Jawblade for anything. But the aquatic criminal had known the risks when he recruited his partner, so there was nothing to do but to press on and hope for the best.

After much too long, Jawblade spotted a glimmer of light ahead. That would be the security beacons active in every hall of the museum— essentially, emergency illumination for anyone who might be working late. Jawblade hadn't considered the possibility that anyone might be putting in overtime at the museum tonight, but if they were, it would be just too bad for them.

They emerged from the pipe into a large aquarium. From Jawblade's research, he knew it held a viper squid from the planet Scylla. While extremely ugly, the creatures weren't as fierce as their name made them sound. If startled, they gave off a cloud of black ink. Jawblade figured this would make for great cover in case a guard walked in early.

The next part of the plan called for Toxic Reapa to use his weapon to cut a hole in the top of the tank, then climb out and start looting. All of this went without a hitch. Jawblade watched with something almost like pride as his partner began smashing display cases and grabbing samples of the most valuable metals in the galaxy.

Everything was going great, and there was no sign of Splitface's Hero Factory. *More than likely that two-faced amateur ran into a couple of cleaning robots and panicked*, thought Jawblade. *Bet on it — there's no such thing as Hero Factory.*

Then Jawblade's head exploded.

Well, not really . . . but he wished it would. The pain he suddenly felt was incredibly intense, so bad that he had to squeeze his eyes shut and remind himself to breathe. It took him several moments to realize that he had not been wounded by any physical blow. No, it was a sound that was making him feel this way.

Jawblade forced one eye open. Standing outside of the tank was one robot in black and yellow armor, holding a weapon of some sort. The sound was coming from the weapon.

What felt like an earthquake rocked the aquarium. Jawblade opened the other eye and saw a robot built like a tank slamming his fist down on the floor. The shock waves had knocked Toxic Reapa off his feet. His weapon was now firing acidic sludge at the ceiling, which Jawblade was certain would come down at any moment.

Jawblade immediately came up with a plan of attack. He would throw himself again and again into the wall of the tank until it shattered, the water inside flooding the entire hall. Free to move around, Jawblade would use his powerful teeth and incredible swimming ability to drive away the attackers, and then he and Toxic Reapa would escape with their loot.

Yes, that was exactly what he would do, Jawblade knew . . . if he were completely dumb.

Facts were facts, and Jawblade had to face them. He didn't know who these two robots were, what else they might be able to do, and if they were out to arrest the two thieves or dismantle them. Finding out the answer to any of those questions might prove very painful. Add to that the simple truth that he owed Toxic Reapa nothing—the walking pollution factory had probably set off an alarm, after all—and Jawblade's course was clear.

He dove for the pipe and made his escape back to the river. If he didn't see Toxic Reapa again, well, no big loss. The important thing was that he had to tell Splitface what he had seen. If these two weren't the same two robots Splitface had seen, the galactic underworld just might be in for trouble.

"The museum isn't going to like that," said Stringer. He was referring to Bulk's having torn up part of the metal flooring in order to wrap it around Toxic Reapa.

"They'd like being robbed a lot less," Bulk answered. "What happened to yours?"

"Disappeared down a hole," said Stringer. "If we'd had a few extra Heroes, we could have covered all the possible exits."

"Give it time," Bulk said. "We will. In the meantime, we've got another occupant for the asteroid. If this keeps up, Hero Factory is going to need a prison of its own pretty soon."

"Ha! I can just see that." Stringer laughed. "Who gets to be the guard?"

"We'll let Stormer do it," Bulk answered, smiling. "He can spend all day telling them how they have no chance because Hero Factory's here. He loves giving that speech."

"Stuck in a cell and having to listen to that? No way," said Stringer. "Hero Factory doesn't torture, remember?"

Over the next several weeks, it seemed that Hero Factory was everywhere. Crimes both minor and spectacular were broken up by Thresher and his team. From the heavily populated worlds of the galactic core to the frontier planets of the rim, no one could predict where a Hero Factory member might show up. In some regions of the galaxy, crime came to a standstill. At least one planetary government fell when Stormer and Von Ness exposed rampant corruption and secret deals with criminals.

It didn't take long for the galactic media to jump on the story. Thresher was all over the news, assuring the public that Hero Factory was around to help keep the average robot safe. Any complaints about a private individual manufacturing Heroes and allowing them to operate all over the galaxy with no real legal authority swiftly died out as the record of Hero Factory successes kept growing. Everywhere you looked, everyone was happy that the new Heroes were on the scene.

Well, almost everyone . . .

In the hideouts and gathering places of the underworld, all the talk was about Hero Factory. Criminals who had never before had to run from the law suddenly feared pulling a robbery or hijacking a freighter, worried that Bulk and Stringer might show up. Thieves who had never once failed on a job were now coming back empty-handed, complaining that Stormer and Von Ness had gotten in their way. There was general agreement that something had to be done, but no one knew what.

Through it all, one master criminal was silent: Black Phantom. No one had seen him or spoken to him in over a month. Rumors were flying that Hero Factory had captured him and was keeping it quiet, or even that he had turned into an informer for Thresher. It was a puzzle to those who knew him, but everyone had worries of their own and no time to worry about a missing crook. There were, after all, a lot of criminals who had gone missing since Hero Factory arrived on the scene.

"If I could just get my hands on that Stormer . . ." Splitface muttered. He was in one of his favorite robot repair shops. Usually a haven for criminals back from rough jobs, tonight it was half-empty.

"He would get his hands on you, too," said Speeda Demon. "Maybe you and Voltix could share a cell."

"I hate Hero Factory," hissed Thornraxx. The insectoid was hanging upside down from the ceiling, one of many annoying habits he had. "Hunt them down. Make them pay."

"Easy for you to say," said Jawblade. "You haven't even tried to steal a handful of bolts from a machine shop in weeks, Thornraxx. I know you heard about that easy haul on Z'Chaya, but you said you were too busy cleaning your nest to do the job. Thresher has you so scared you might as well retire."

There was a long, awkward silence. Jawblade had just put into words what they were all thinking. If they couldn't find some way to deal with Hero Factory, it might be time for all of them to find another line of work.

"Don't start packing just yet."

The voice belonged to Black Phantom. The other criminals greeted him with a nod or a shrug, then went back to brooding. The tall thief smiled and walked over to Splitface.

"What's the matter? You always say you think twice as fast as any other crook, but you can't plot your way out of this?"

He turned to Speeda Demon, saying, "You're swifter than any robot out there, but you're cooling your jets in here instead of going out and taking what you want."

Black Phantom glanced up at Thornraxx. "As

for you . . . well, I don't even know what you are, so just keep hanging there."

"Listen, BP, no one has any idea where you've been all this time, and now you come here dumping on us," said Splitface. "Why should we care what you say? I don't see you pulling any big jobs and taking on Thresher and the rest. You been hiding under a rock or something?"

Black Phantom walked to the head of the table so he could address all four criminals. "Where have I been? I've been getting to know the enemy. The Heroes are bright and effective, but they aren't very good at being sneaky yet. None of them thought to keep an eye out for someone watching them, learning their moves, finding their weaknesses."

"And what did you find?" asked Speeda Demon, not sounding very interested. He had always considered Black Phantom to be all talk.

"First, I have something to say to all of you," was the reply. "You've gotten soft. You've gotten slow. You're so used to getting your own way that you run and hide at the first sign of someone standing up to you." Black Phantom glared at Splitface and Jawblade. "You even desert your partners in the middle of a job. Is that how the top criminals in the galaxy behave?"

"Okay, you're the class of the underworld, for whatever that's worth. We'll steal you a medal later on," said Speeda Demon. "Just make your point."

"Point! Point!" chimed in Thornraxx.

"Fine," answered Black Phantom. "Hero Factory is successful because they work as a team. If we want to beat them, then we have to work as a team, too. We have to back each other up, work together, match up our strengths and weaknesses the same way they do."

Splitface laughed derisively. "Maybe we can all sit around and sing songs, too, just to show how well we get along."

Black Phantom was on Splitface in two quick strides. He kicked the chair out from under Splitface, sending the surprised robot to the floor.

"You've got two choices: my plan or a cell in

some asteroid prison," growled Black Phantom. "Which is it going to be?"

"Enough," said Jawblade. "Keep talking. We're all listening."

Black Phantom gave Splitface an idle kick as he returned to the head of the table. "We beat Hero Factory with their own tricks. They have their Alpha Team . . . we will be a Legion of Darkness."

"Shouldn't a Legion have more guys?" asked Speeda Demon.

"Right. That's why our first mission is going to be breaking Voltix and Toxic Reapa out of jail."

The other four villains all looked at one another as if to say, "He's crazy." Nobody liked either of those two criminals enough to risk their freedom to get them out of prison.

Black Phantom sensed what they were thinking. "It's not about whether we like each other or not. We're a team now. It's time we started acting like it."

"All right," said Speeda Demon. "So just how do you propose we pull off this mission of yours?"

Black Phantom smiled. "Simple. We're going to do the same thing Hero Factory would do: We're going to build a Hero."

Splitface, Speeda Demon, and Black Phantom crouched on a ridge overlooking a large manufacturing plant. It was well past midnight and the moons had ducked behind clouds, but all three criminals had set their optic sensors for night vision. They could easily make out the few guards near the front and rear entrances, as well as the hover vehicles entering and leaving the shipping docks. All in all, it looked like a normal night at any factory in the galaxy.

"I don't get it," said Splitface, his voice sounding like gravel being ground up. "Why are we here?"

"That's a Makuro plant, isn't it?" asked Speeda Demon. "He's the one behind Hero Factory?"

"Right," said Black Phantom. "Look at what they're loading into those vehicles."

Speeda Demon took a step forward and

peered down. A column of four-armed robots was marching into a hover vehicle, then turning and sitting down in the rear of the transport. Other than their yellow armor, there was nothing particularly unusual about them.

"Worker robots, so what?"

"So we're going to steal one," said Black Phantom.

Down below, the last in a line of hover vehicles took off. When it was about three hundred feet off the ground, Thornraxx shot down from the sky. The insectoid robot landed on the right wing of the vehicle, throwing the craft off balance. It banked sharply to the left, heading straight for the hillside where the three criminals were standing.

"Duck!" yelled Splitface.

"Relax," said Black Phantom. "He knows what he's doing."

As they watched, Thornraxx made his way to the cockpit. His stinger made short work of the robot pilot, and he quickly took over the controls. After righting the craft, he brought it in for a landing just beyond the hill.

"How did he learn to pilot like that?" asked Speeda Demon.

"He flies," said Black Phantom, "so it came easy to him. I didn't put him on the team for his looks."

Thornraxx was already buzzing around the downed hovercraft when his three partners arrived. Black Phantom led the two dozen industrial robots from the vehicle. Then he turned to Splitface and Speeda Demon, saying, "Smash it. Make it look like it crashed."

The two criminals took to their task with glee. Meanwhile, Black Phantom was tinkering with the controls on the robots. When he was done, all but one marched off into the night.

"Escaping? Escaping!" said Thornraxx.

"No," Black Phantom assured him, "just scattering. They'll wander for a few miles in random directions. Then their power sources will run down, thanks to my sabotage, and they'll drop wherever they're standing."

"I get it," said Speeda Demon, smiling. "When

Makuro's recovery team searches for them, they'll be all over. So if one is missing, it will be assumed that that one wandered someplace way far off and can't be found. They probably won't even report it."

Black Phantom patted the back of the robot he had "rescued." "And no one will be looking for XT4, here. Thanks to Mr. Makuro and his manufacturing plant, we have just what we need to destroy Hero Factory."

can't believe this!" fumed Stringer, walking rapidly down the hallway from the meeting room. "Is this what being a Hero is all about?"

Stormer, coming the other way, reached out a hand to stop him. "What's the matter?"

Stringer showed Stormer his datapad. "We got new missions from Thresher. Bulk and Von Ness are supposed to meet a freight convoy and act as escorts, while you and I go to some backwater world on the rim and watch over a relocation of some mining robots from one region to the other. What's heroic about that?"

Stormer looked over the orders. Stringer was right, the missions seemed pretty dull. But they couldn't always be chasing down dangerous criminals. There were others services Hero Factory could and should perform for the galaxy. If Thresher said this was what the team should be doing, Stormer was willing to accept that.

Unfortunately, it was impossible to ask Thresher for more details. He and Zib, the technical wizard who oversaw the operations of Hero Factory, had left to investigate a hovercraft crash near one of Mr. Makuro's companies.

"Where's Bulk?"

"Left already," said Stringer. "We better go, too, or this exciting adventure might start without us."

The trip to the galactic rim took a long time, even in the new Hero craft Zib had provided. Stringer spent most of his time playing music while Stormer studied the Hero Factory manual. After several hours, Stringer said, "You really find that stuff fascinating, don't you?"

"Not fascinating, but important," answered Stormer. "Our lives might depend on knowing all this someday, or maybe the lives of innocents. We need to know what to do in any situation."

Stringer slumped down in the copilot's chair and put his feet up on the console. "You never will, friend. The galaxy is a big place, full of things none of us could imagine. Right now, there could be some new kind of trouble brewing, just waiting for us to walk into it."

"There are no new kinds of trouble," Stormer said. He punched up an image of Black Phantom on the console. "Only new kinds of troublemakers."

Stringer sat up and did a fast scan of Black Phantom's profile and record. When he was done, he said, "Why does this one worry you any more than the others?"

Stormer thought about it for a minute before he answered. "Because he's off the grid. No one has seen or heard from him in weeks, at least according to our sources. His type doesn't lie so low unless they're up to something big."

"Maybe Hero Factory scared him off," Stringer suggested, with a laugh.

"I'm not so sure we're scaring anyone . . . yet," said Stormer. "Inconveniencing them, maybe. Puzzling them. But they don't know whether to be afraid of us or not."

"I'd be afraid of us," said Stringer.

"Why?"

"'Cause we don't know what we're doing. We're zipping around the galaxy sticking our noses into whatever we like, hoping we can tell the good guys from the bad guys. One of these days, we're going to get it wrong . . . and that will be the end of us, one way or the other."

"Try not to be such a pessimist," said Stormer. "Seriously, if you don't believe in what we're doing—"

"I didn't say I don't believe in it," Stringer interrupted. "I just think maybe there's a reason no one tried to do it before. Or maybe they did, and it ended up so badly that no one wants to talk about it."

Stormer chose to ignore Stringer's last comment. "Planet's down below."

It was a pretty typical mining world. All of the

trees and other natural features had long since been blasted away or plowed under, leaving just an ugly rock fit only to drill bigger and deeper holes in. According to the mission briefing, one area in the northeastern region had become so geologically unstable that the miners had to be evacuated and put to work elsewhere. It was what Bulk usually called a "robot-sitting" mission.

Stormer brought the Hero craft in for a landing. As they emerged, they saw scores of mining robots hard at work carrying picks and shovels into the mine and others carrying ore back out. None of them paid any attention to the new arrivals.

Stringer noticed a slightly larger robot with a black stripe running down his right arm. He would be part of the special class of forebots, whose job it was to keep an eye on the workers. The Hero walked up to him and said, "We're from Hero Factory, here to supervise the move."

The robot's expression turned blank. "What move?"

"The one that involves saving all your miners

from being swallowed up by a sinkhole. You know, *that* move."

The forebot checked his datapad. "No, I got nothing about 'sinkholes', 'swallowed up', or 'moves' on my schedule. Gotta stick to the schedule, right? Pretty sure you guys aren't on my schedule, either. So why are you here? Spies for the boss?"

"Stormer, we have a little problem," Stringer called over his shoulder.

"I told him we'd meet our quota if he'd send better mining robots," the forebot continued. "This bunch couldn't find a barrel of duradium if they tripped over it. But do I get any help? No. I just hear about missed quotas and how I better start doing my job or I'll be monitoring waste disposal systems next week."

Stormer approached. "What's going on?"

"Are you sure we got the right coordinates?" asked Stringer.

"Thresher doesn't make mistakes like that."

"Then something else is wrong, because my

friend here doesn't know anything about any move. See if you can reach Hero Factory and find out if there's an update."

Stormer activated his helmet radio but got only static. He frowned. There was nothing on this world that should have interfered with communications, and no solar storms in the area. That left one other possibility.

"Come with me, Stringer," he said as calmly as he could.

The two Heroes walked several yards away from the mine. "I think our communications are being jammed," said Stormer. "Listen, did you get this mission directly from Thresher?"

"No, he posted it to my datapad. He and Zib had already left."

Stormer scanned the area as he said, "What if it didn't come from him? What if our system has been hacked?"

"Now who's being a pessimist? Zib said our security was—"

Stormer cut him off. "Everything's new, and

a lot of it is untested. Maybe somebody found a way in and is sending us off on false missions."

"So they could do what?"

"That," said Stormer, pointing behind Stringer.

The Hero turned to see dozens of mining robots, each armed with a turbo jackhammer, and all of them advancing toward Stormer and Stringer. They were not coming to throw a welcome party.

"Trap," said Stringer.

"What gave it away? Let's get back to the Hero craft!"

The two robots turned to run. As they did so, they saw that more mining robots had moved between them and their ship. They were surrounded.

"Okay," said Stringer. "They're armed, but not that well-armed. There's just a lot of them."

"What do you figure the odds are?"

"I stopped counting when I hit eight to one," Stringer answered, smiling. "Hey, be careful when you start using your launcher. You know how these mining colonies are — you break it, you buy it."

Stormer spotted the forebot trying frantically to get the miners to turn around. The worker robots completely ignored him. They weren't on a general rampage then, but were rather a weapon aimed right at the two Heroes.

"Get ready for it," said Stringer. "We can try to fight our way to the ship, before the ones behind us cut us down."

"Nice working with you," replied Stormer.

The robots approached from all sides, jack-hammers revving. Stormer and Stringer braced themselves for combat. They knew they had no chance against so many opponents, but for the sake of Hero Factory's reputation, they would go down fighting.

Then an amazing thing happened. A beam of light flashed from a nearby pile of rock and struck the ground in front of the oncoming robots, instantly carving a trench that ran for a hundred yards. Two more light beams hit to the left and right of the Heroes, cutting off the robots on either side. That left only the ones in front of the Hero craft for Stormer and Stringer to deal with.

It was a quick fight. With the odds so whittled down, Stormer's power blasts and Stringer's sonic beam shut down the mining robots. Both were able to make it back to the ship, but Stringer stopped Stormer before they went in.

"Somebody saved us back there," he said. "I don't know about you, but I'd like to know who."

"I think we're about to find out," Stormer answered.

Clambering down the pile of rock was a four-armed industrial robot with yellow armor. Mounted on its arm was a device Stormer recognized as a laser slicer, no doubt the weapon responsible for the trenches.

"Do you know him?" asked Stormer.

"New to me," said Stringer.

The robot walked up to them and stopped about three feet from where they were standing. "I am XT4. When it was discovered that you had been lured to this planet under false pretenses,

I was dispatched by Hero Factory to assist you."

"Excuse me, just who are you?" asked Stormer.

"I am XT4. I was activated in the Assembly Tower yesterday. I am the newest member of Alpha Team."

Stormer glanced at Stringer, who shrugged. Neither of them had heard about any new recruits.

"Thanks for the save, but . . . is there some way you can prove you are who you say you are?" asked Stringer.

"Contact Hero Factory. They can confirm," replied XT4 in a flat, monotone voice.

"Stringer, I need to show you something in the ship," said Stormer, guiding his partner toward the Hero craft. "XT4, you stay here and . . . um . . . look for clues."

When they were inside the ship, Stormer said, "We can't contact base. Maybe he knows that?"

"Or maybe he's what he says he is," Stringer replied. "If they knew we needed help, and Bulk and Von Ness weren't available . . . anyway, we can't leave him here, regardless. He has to come with us."

"I know," said Stormer. "I just wish I didn't hate the idea quite so much."

Not far away, Black Phantom watched things play out from a safe hiding place. He was watching as Stringer and Stormer invited XT4 into the ship, followed shortly thereafter by the Hero craft blasting off into space.

The villain smiled. Everything was going according to plan. XT4 had been reprogrammed to believe himself a member of Hero Factory, and he would keep on believing it until the proper signal was transmitted. Having picked up a little electronics knowledge by watching this process, Speeda Demon had been able to reprogram the mining robots extremely quickly. They were ready and waiting when the Heroes arrived, courtesy of the fake mission Black Phantom had plugged into the command system.

Now XT4 was on his way back to Hero Factory. He would be key to breaking Voltix and

Toxic Reapa out of jail, not to mention all the knowledge he might gain from Mr. Makuro's facility. This would be the first blow to Hero Factory's reputation.

But it won't be the last, thought Black Phantom. *The last one comes when their little team lies in ruins.*

By the time Stormer, Stringer, and XT4 made it back to Hero Factory, Bulk and Von Ness had already returned from their mission. Theirs, it seemed, was legitimate, if boring. The freight convoy had reached its destination without incident. The shipmasters had made sure everyone knew Hero Factory was providing security, and that had frightened off the local pirates.

They listened with interest to Stringer's story. Von Ness, especially, looked troubled by it.

"Our enemies are getting more organized," he commented. "That trap took time and effort to set up."

"But one extra Hero blew the whole thing apart," said Bulk.

"That was . . . convenient," replied Von Ness.

"Stormer is checking XT4 out now," said Stringer. "We should know the score in a few moments."

In the command center, Stormer was indeed getting ready to punch in the data on XT4 into the Assembly Tower manifest program. If he had been produced recently, he would appear in the listing. If not . . .

He had left XT4 in a secure area. There were no computer consoles or datapads in the room, or any port that would allow the new "Hero" access to Hero Factory information. Stormer figured he had a few minutes before XT4 got suspicious.

In the other room, XT4 had other things on his mind. A passing ore freighter that had been hijacked by Splitface had just transmitted the signal that initiated his second layer of programming.

XT4 was now prepared to actively contribute to the destruction of Hero Factory. His computer brain did a swift analysis of the power readings in the secure room and reached a conclusion.

Stormer had made an error. This room was for guests, not prisoners. It was designed to restrict access to the main computer system, but it did not take into account someone cutting a hole in the wall and tapping into the internal data conduits. That was just what XT4 proceeded to do, using his laser slicer and one of his four arms.

From there, it was simple. First, he downloaded anything and everything on Hero Factory and its Heroes. Once that was done, he rerouted the security system so that it would ignore him but treat the Heroes as intruders. As soon as that was completed to his satisfaction, XT4 triggered a security alert.

The list scrolled by quickly. Stormer could see that no new Heroes had been produced in the last week, let alone dispatched. XT4 was a fake.

He was about to contact Stringer and the others when the alarm began to sound and the lights in the room started flashing. Before Stormer could check for the source of the alarm signal, a stun beam from the ceiling knocked him out.

Stormer's circuits shut down, not knowing that the same thing was now happening to Bulk, Stringer, and Von Ness. . . .

Aboard his scout ship, Black Phantom smiled. He had just received the signal from XT4 that the Heroes were incapacitated and the plan was proceeding.

It would, of course, have been easy to attack Hero Factory now and wreck the Heroes and the entire facility. That was certainly what Splitface and Speeda Demon wanted to do. But "easy to attack" was not the same as "easy to win." Hero Factory's security system was designed to stun intruders, not destroy them, so Stormer and the rest might reboot at any time. If they did wake up, it would mean fighting them on their home ground. Even with the villains having the advantage of surprise, the odds would still be with Alpha Team.

No, this operation had to be done with precision and patience. The next step was to get the Legion of Darkness up to full strength. Then it would be time to deal with the so-called Heroes.

Black Phantom flipped on the comm switch. "Splitface, proceed with Plan Omega. Change course and be prepared to back up XT4 should he need it."

"Got it," came Splitface's reply a moment later.

Black Phantom entered a new course into his nav computer and started after XT4. He intended to be on the scene for every part of this plan's execution. Plus, he hadn't been to a good prison break in years. . . .

Stormer abruptly sat up. His reboot had been so sudden it took him a moment to realize where he was and what had just happened. The alarm had shut off and the stunner had retracted back into the ceiling. That didn't explain why it had gone off in the first place or why it had targeted Heroes.

He did a fast sensor scan. Yes, XT4 was gone. Worse, the hangar bay log showed that a Hero craft had made an unauthorized departure a few minutes before. It didn't take a genius to figure out who must have stolen it.

"Computer, plot projected course for Hero craft One and display," Stormer said.

The thinking machine whirred for a few seconds, and then the screen lit up with a star chart bisected by a flashing red line. Based on its present course and speed, the stolen ship was headed for a big hunk of rock called Asteroid J-54. Also known as "the Stone," it was the largest prison in the sector and home to every criminal Hero Factory had captured so far.

Why do I think he's not just headed there for Visiting Day? Stormer said to himself.

He slammed his hand down on the comm

button. "Stringer, Bulk, Von Ness—anybody—please respond."

The speaker crackled. "This is Stringer. What hit us?"

"Our guest was more talented than I expected, I guess," Stormer replied. "Thresher is going to have me scrubbing floors when he finds out. Head to the hangar bay—things are about to get much worse."

XT4 brought the Hero craft in for a landing on Asteroid J-54. As expected, the ship's configuration was recognized by the prison's automatic security system and so it was not fired upon. Once on the ground, the villainous robot departed the ship and marched to the main gate. Two security robots waited there.

"Identification," said one of the guards.

"I am from Hero Factory, here to interrogate prisoner Toxic Reapa," answered XT4.

"Identification," the guard repeated.

"Ah, yes, I have it right here," said XT4, extending his right arm.

When the guard glanced down, XT4 triggered his laser slicer, cutting cleanly through the security robot's command circuits. Before the other guard could react, XT4 did the same thing to him. Both guards were still functioning, but commands from their central computers could no longer reach their bodies. They were both just so much useless metal until they could be repaired.

XT4 stepped past them and through the main gate. Thanks to the information he had downloaded from Hero Factory, he knew Voltix and Toxic Reapa were in adjoining cells. Voltix's cell was made of a special nonconductive plastic, which rendered his electrical powers useless. Toxic Reapa was enclosed in a dome that was impervious to the acidic sludge he fired. Fortunately for them, Hero Factory's main computers contained the access codes needed to free them.

He walked quickly but calmly through the prison corridors, ignoring the calls from other inmates. Any guards who tried to get in his way were swiftly incapacitated. Industrial robots were designed to be able to focus on any set task to the exclusion of all else. XT4 would not allow himself to be distracted from rescuing the two prisoners he was there to retrieve.

When he found the right cells, XT4 stopped and turned. "I am XT4," he announced. "I have come to free the prisoners designated Voltix and Toxic Reapa."

Voltix glanced at his neighbor. "This smells like a trap." He turned back to his would-be rescuer. "What's in it for you, tinhead?"

"Please listen to this prerecorded message," said XT4. When he opened his mouth again, Black Phantom's voice came out.

"Reapa, Voltix—you know who I am and what I stand for. I'm forming a team to wipe out Hero Factory before they cause us any more trouble. XT4 works for me. So do a lot of other professionals you know. I want you on the team—that is why I arranged this little party.

Of course, if you prefer to keep working on your own, I can have XT4 leave you here. I'm sure you'll be back out in the spaceways in ten or twenty years."

Voltix glanced at Toxic Reapa, with a "What have we got to lose?" shrug. Neither of them knew Black Phantom all that well, but he must have had some kind of a plan if he had organized this prison break.

"Sure, we're in," said Toxic Reapa. "Now get us out of here."

Two Hero craft emerged from hyperspace near Asteroid J-54. Bulk and Von Ness were aboard one, Stormer and Stringer the other. The first sight to greet their eyes was an old ore freighter in orbit around the prison.

"What's that doing there?" asked Stringer.

"Nothing good," Stormer replied. He switched on the comm. "Bulk, you and Von Ness head for the surface. Sensors show the stolen Hero craft is already on the ground. Stringer and I are going to check out this freighter."

"Got it," Bulk radioed back. The other Hero craft broke away and headed for the asteroid.

"How do you want to play this?" Stringer asked. "Polite or rude?"

"Let's try polite and see what it gets us. Are you reading any weapons systems on that tub?"

"Negative." Stringer activated the ship-to-ship radio. "Attention, freighter, this is Hero craft Two from Hero Factory. Please identify yourself and state your business here."

The response was dead silence.

Stringer tried again, this time sounding a little more annoyed. "Freighter, this is Hero craft Two. You are in what is almost certainly an unauthorized orbit around a prison world. Please identity yourself, or be considered hostile."

That got a reaction. The freighter broke orbit and slowly began to move toward the Hero craft. Built for carrying capacity, not for speed, it moved through the sea of space like a sick whale.

"You're sure they're not armed?"

"Sure, I'm sure," said Stringer. "Nervous?"

"They are on a collision course," Stormer reminded him.

"At that speed?" Stringer laughed. "We could go back to Hero Factory, have lunch, and come back here and that pile of tin still wouldn't have reached this spot."

"Get the shields up anyway," said Stormer. "I've been fooled once today. It's not going to happen twice."

Black Phantom saw the freighter moving on his scope and shook his head. What was Splitface thinking? He got his chance to ask a moment later when Splitface and Speeda Demon suddenly materialized inside his scout ship.

"Who knew?" Splitface said, smiling. "A rusted out old hulk like that has a working trans-mat beam."

"You really ought to keep your shields up,

Phantom," said Speeda Demon. "Anyone could drop in."

Black Phantom glared at them both. "What are you doing here? Your orders were to help XT4 if he needed it."

"Watch your mouth, pal," Splitface growled. "I don't remember voting for you to be boss. Speeda and me, we came up with some new orders."

"What did you do?" asked Black Phantom, already dreading the answer.

"Rigged the engines to explode," Speeda Demon answered, proudly. "Soon as it gets close to the Hero craft, boom!"

Black Phantom used language under his breath that polite robots would never say. Then he slammed his hand down on the control panel. "So you take out one or two Heroes, then what? Makuro makes more and they track us all halfway across the galaxy for revenge. My way—"

"—is too slow," shot back Splitface. "You want to bore the Heroes into submission? Fine. I want 'em in little bits. You do things your way, and I'll do 'em mine."

"This is why we lose," muttered Black Phantom. "No teamwork. Fine, since you rust-for-brains have started this, I might as well finish it. Is the crew still on board the freighter?"

"Nah, we ditched them on an asteroid a ways back," Splitface answered.

"Good, they would just complicate matters," said Black Phantom as he started working the cockpit controls.

"What are you doing?" asked Speeda Demon.

"That freighter is moving at a space snail's pace," the leader of the Legion explained. "It will be a cinch for the Hero craft to outrun it. Unless we keep them busy just long enough for the ship to blow. . . ."

Splitface grinned at Speeda Demon. They'd make a real villain out of this guy yet.

5

Bulk and Von Ness exited the Hero craft, ready for trouble. They found it almost immediately.

Even from a distance, it was obvious that the two guards at the gate were just propped up there. Someone had already taken them out. Who that someone was became obvious when XT4 came walking out of the prison, with Toxic Reapa and Voltix right behind him.

"Oh no they don't," said Bulk. He tore a chunk of rock out of the ground and threw it so that it landed right in front of the escaping villains.

"Turn around and go back," Von Ness advised. "His aim is usually a lot better than that."

Toxic Reapa fired a blast of sludge, which ate through the rock in a matter of seconds. Voltix and XT4 had already taken cover and were hurling electric bolts and laser beams at the Heroes.

This was what Bulk and Von Ness had trained for. Bulk's missile weapon turned XT4's hiding spot into a pile of rubble, while Von Ness's gravity weapon slammed Toxic Reapa to the ground. Voltix unleashed a barrage of electricity that temporarily drove the Heroes back. When the lightning storm subsided, they saw the three villains retreating back into the prison.

"I don't see any villain team," grumbled Voltix to XT4. "All I see is you—and if it weren't for me, I'd be seeing you captured by Hero Factory."

"A momentary setback," said XT4. "The Heroes arrived 3.67 minutes earlier than estimated, indicating my calculations of the stun beam's effectiveness were off by .001."

"Great," said Toxic Reapa. "Only we're back

in prison again, and I thought the point was to get out of here."

XT4 spotted what he was looking for, one of the wall-mounted security panels. "We will all get out of here," he assured Toxic Reapa. "And I do mean *all*."

A shot from his laser slicer cut through the security panel. An instant later, all the doors in this wing of the prison had flown open. Inmates began to pour into the corridor, heading for freedom.

"Estimate: The two Heroes will be overwhelmed by the escaping prisoners in approximately 2.346 minutes. They will cease to be any threat to our escape at that time."

"Meaning . . . ?" asked Voltix.

XT4 looked at him as if the answer should have been obvious. "They will cease to be a threat because they will cease . . . to be."

Stringer had called up a schematic of the ore freighter on his screen. Two things stood out for him: There was no sign of any crew on board, and two sectors in the center of the ship were flashing red.

"Oh boy," he said quietly. "Stormer, we've got trouble."

"What kind?"

Stringer pointed at the screen. "The freighter's engines are overloading. It's about to go ka-boom right in our faces."

"Then let's move!" Stormer ordered.

Stringer triggered the aft thrusters and began to back the Hero craft away from the oncoming freighter. They had put only a little distance between them and the larger ship when the Hero craft was rocked by an explosion on its port side.

"Company!" yelled Stringer. "Looks like a scout ship!"

"Hail them!"

When Stringer signaled that communication had been established, Stormer pressed the "Send" switch. "This is Preston Stormer, representing Hero Factory. We are here in pursuit of a dangerous fugitive. Cease all hostile action and identify yourselves."

The ship shuddered as another energy bolt hit the shields. Then the radio crackled as a message was received. "This is Black Phantom, representing the Legion of Darkness. Your friends on the asteroid are in a lot of trouble, Stormer, but don't worry—you won't be around long enough to see what happens to them."

"I could do this all day," said Bulk as he threw boulder after boulder at the gate of the prison. He had spent the last fifteen minutes building a wall where the entrance had been, hoping to at least slow the escaping prisoners down.

"Really?" asked Von Ness.

Bulk looked at his partner as if he had just tumbled out of the Assembly Tower backward. "Um, no. Plus, I'm not sure if this is going to hold them even for a couple of minutes. We need a better plan."

"I have one," Von Ness said, grinning. "Watch."

He turned his gravity weapon on the pile of stone, making each boulder super-heavy and dense. It took a lot of power to do the job, but he felt certain it would buy them time.

"These rocks just became much harder to shatter," Von Ness reported. "They can still get through them, but not easily. I think I know what they'll do, and we should be prepared."

Within a few minutes, they were in position. Someone was pounding on the rocks from the other side. Little by little, the pounding noise came closer. Finally, a narrow wedge of rock fell free, opening an exit from the prison, though only wide enough for one robot to pass through at a time.

As the first inmate emerged from the stone tunnel, he was met with Bulk blocking the way.

"Nah, you're too small," said the Hero. "I'm throwing you back."

With that, Bulk slammed the inmate and sent him staggering back into the tunnel. There he collided with the prisoners behind him, causing a chain reaction as they toppled over each other. As soon as they righted themselves and tried to make another escape, Bulk would bash whoever came out first and create another pileup.

"You know, a robot could get to like this," Bulk said to himself around the fifth time. "Von Ness gave me the easy job. I hope he knows what he's doing."

Right about then, Von Ness was feeling the same way. . . .

Stormer's mind raced. Legion of Darkness? What was that? It was never mentioned in any Hero Factory files, he was certain of that.

"So, Black Phantom," he said, "you and XT4 are in this together?"

Black Phantom laughed. "Oh, it's much more than just us two. There are a lot of people who hate Hero Factory. You might say we decided to form a club."

Not good, thought Stormer. Asteroid J-54 was loaded with criminals, big-time and small-time, put away by Hero Factory in recent weeks. If Black Phantom was here on a recruiting drive, Alpha Team could be in for serious trouble.

"Be careful," Stormer said, doing his best to sound intimidating. "No one has beaten Hero Factory yet."

"No one has really tried," replied Black Phantom. "Everyone has been too busy saying, 'Who are those robots?' That's the difference — I don't care who you are, what you stand for, or where you're from — I only care about where you're going."

Stringer tried to navigate the Hero craft away from both the scout ship and the freighter. But Black Phantom was no slouch at the controls, and he kept darting in and out, forcing the Hero craft back toward the floating explosive that was the ore freighter.

"We're running out of time," Stringer said to Stormer. "We need to get past him or go through him."

Stormer activated the comm again. "What do you want, Black Phantom?"

"What do I want? I want Hero Factory in ruins," answered Black Phantom. "I want this whole experiment of Makuro's to end in such utter failure that no one will try it again for at least a few centuries. I was planning to play with all of you a while longer, but my colleagues aren't known for their patience."

Stormer cut off communication. He turned to Stringer, saying, "Go through him."

"Gotcha, boss," Stringer said, smiling.

The Hero craft shot forward, maneuvered by the expert hands of Stringer. It dove under the scout ship and came up on the other side, putting Black Phantom's vessel between it and the freighter. When the scout ship tried to slip past to relative safety, Stringer matched the move and blocked it.

"Stalemate, Black Phantom," Stormer radioed. "If that ship blows, it takes us all out."

"I don't believe in stalemates, Hero," Black Phantom replied. "I only play to win."

In the next instant, Stringer and Stormer watched unbelieving as the scout ship broke apart. The wings and tail drifted off into space, leaving only the small cockpit in which Black Phantom, Splitface, and Speeda Demon sat. Before Stringer could react, the cockpit section shot past at an incredible rate of speed and disappeared.

"I didn't know they could do that," said Stringer. "Did you know they could do that?"

"Worry about that later," snapped Stormer. "Get us out of here!"

Stringer hit the thrusters and the ship surged ahead, just as the engines of the ore freighter reached the point of no return. The old vessel went up in a massive explosion that swallowed up the fleeing Hero craft in its fiery maw.

Von Ness completed his climb up to the roof of the prison. He was certain that XT4, Toxic Reapa, and Voltix would be coming out this way, assuming that he and Bulk would be busy down below with the other escapees.

It would feel good to be right, but . . . he wasn't thrilled at the thought of facing all three villains by himself. Sure, he was one of the more powerful Heroes, but it would only take one lucky blast by any of the three and he would be a pile of junk.

It was time to call for backup.

Activating his helmet radio, Von Ness broadcast, "Hero craft Two, do you read? Mass prison escape. Require assistance."

There was no answer. That didn't make sense. After all, Stormer and Stringer were just supposed to be checking out that ore freighter, which had probably broken down and gotten stuck here. How long could that take?

"Hero craft Two, come in!" he repeated, more urgently this time. "This is Von Ness. Bulk and I are in serious trouble down here and—"

The sky was suddenly split by a burst of light. Almost against his will, Von Ness looked up, using his hand to shield his optic sensors as he did so. In that moment, he knew what it meant to lose all hope.

Something had exploded in space, something very big . . . and, he was sure, it had taken Hero craft 2, Stormer, and Stringer with it.

6

ention outer space to someone and certain qualities come to mind right away. Space is big; it's cold; most of it is empty of any matter. It's less of a place than it is an enigma, one that can be conquered with great spaceships, yet one that can also take a terrible vengeance if one of those fragile metal vehicles runs into trouble.

Most of all, space is quiet.

Here in space, battles are fought, stars explode, entire planetary systems get wiped out, all without any noise at all. In space, destruction comes without even a whisper.

Aboard Hero craft 2, it was also very quiet.

Two Heroes lay stretched out on the hard deck, unmoving. Whatever alarms might normally have been sounding were too badly damaged to make a noise. The ship itself was almost as dark as it was silent, with only dim emergency lighting illuminating the interior.

A visitor to the ship would have gotten the impression that nothing was left alive there, but that would not have been accurate. There was one panel on the console that was still very much active. It was a small, square section of the controls that flashed red only under a particular set of circumstances. In fact, it came to life only to announce that everything else was about to expire.

It was the Life Support Beacon, which activated when all heat and air systems were shutting down in the ship. The numbing cold of outer space was seeping into the Hero craft now, about to freeze Stringer and Stormer solid.

Perhaps, then, it was for the best that the systems of the two Heroes had not yet rebooted. There was, after all, no way they could save themselves.

Von Ness was still trying to process the idea of Stormer and Stringer being destroyed when the roof nearby caved in. Emerging from the resulting hole were XT4, Toxic Reapa, and Voltix.

"Oh, look," said Voltix. "One little Hero, all by himself."

"Bet he's lonely," said Toxic Reapa. "Let's send him back to his pals . . . in pieces."

"I fail to understand," XT4 interrupted, "this need for intimidating banter prior to a fight. Our purpose is to escape. This Hero stands opposed to that purpose and so must be eliminated. Why is additional conversation required?"

"Because," answered Toxic Reapa, "it's fun to watch the big, brave Heroes shaking in their boots."

Von Ness readied himself for battle. "You'll never see that day. Hero Factory put you behind bars once and we can do it again."

"'We?'" asked Voltix. He looked all around. "I don't see any 'we,' just you—unless you Heroes have added invisibility to your powers now?"

Von Ness didn't answer. He knew the situation. With Bulk busy on the ground and Hero craft 2 lost, it was going to be stand or fall for him — probably fall — here on this rooftop. He didn't want things to end here, not on some crummy rooftop on a prison asteroid.

"We are wasting time," XT4 said.

"Maybe," Toxic Reapa replied, looking closely at Von Ness. "Yeah, and maybe not. How come the Hero here hasn't attacked yet? Maybe he's having second thoughts?"

Toxic Reapa took three steps forward, then stopped. "Hey, you! Are you going to fight, or what?"

"Knock it off, TR," said Voltix. "He doesn't have to fight if he doesn't want to."

I don't? thought Von Ness. *Of course I do! I'm a Hero. They're villains. It's my job. But . . . I never asked for this job. I just got created and told this is what I would be doing. No one asked if it was what I wanted to do.*

"Listen, friend," Voltix continued. "We've got

nothing to fight about. We're all robots here, right? Nobody's better than anybody else. Now, what do you have to gain by trying to stop us? We're just going to defeat you and leave you for your bulky buddy to find. Sure, you'll be able to talk about how you tried your best to stop us . . . you can talk about it the whole time you're on your back in the repair shop. Or . . ."

"Or . . . ?" Von Ness wasn't even aware he was saying the word until it emerged from his mouth.

"Or you look the other way," Voltix said quietly. "You let us go, we let you go. Nobody gets hurt. Nobody ever has to know."

"What about Bulk?" said Von Ness. A part of him couldn't believe he was negotiating with these criminals, but a bigger part couldn't see any reason not to. Hey, even if they escaped, Thresher would track them down eventually . . . wouldn't he?

"Sure, we'll leave the big guy alone, too," Voltix assured him. "All we want is to get off this rock. What do you say?"

Von Ness thought about it. He remembered Voltix's electrical bolts, Toxic Reapa's radioactive sludge, and XT4's laser slicer. With his gravity weapon, he might stop one, maybe two, but the third one would get him. And all for what? Mr. Makuro's personal crusade?

"All right," Von Ness said, gaze dropping to the ground. "Get going, the three of you. I never saw you. But if Bulk spots you, you're on your own."

The three villains headed for the rear of the prison roof and disappeared over the side. Von Ness watched them go. He still had time to try to stop them or at least broadcast a warning to Bulk. But he did nothing.

A few minutes later, Bulk appeared on the roof. He looked battered and exhausted, but still managed a smile. "They won't try that again for a while. I ought to visit this rock more often. Heck of a workout they give you here!"

Bulk's eyes went to the hole on the roof, and then to Von Ness. "What happened? I thought you said XT4 would be sure to try to get out this way."

"And I was right," said Von Ness, never looking

at his partner. "But they were already gone when I got here. I . . . never saw them."

"Well, what are you standing there for?" Bulk demanded. "There might still be time to catch them!"

That hope was shot down as the familiar roar of a Hero craft filled the air. XT4 was escaping in his stolen ship with Toxic Reapa and Voltix.

Bulk didn't hesitate. He charged for the edge of the roof, and scrambled down the wall, with Von Ness behind him. They were halfway to their Hero craft when they spotted the green ooze that covered it. As they drew closer, they saw that the hull was ruined thanks to damage done by Toxic Reapa. This particular Hero craft would never fly again.

"Wow," Bulk said. His shoulders were slumped in defeat. "I don't think I want to be there when Stormer finds out about this."

"I don't think we need to worry about that," said Von Ness sadly.

A lone Hero craft approached Asteroid J-54. Its pilot noted the wreckage of the freighter and the lack of any signal from any other Hero Factory ship. He feared the worst.

They were—are—*my team,* thought Thresher. *I should have been here with them, instead of running what amounted to an errand for Mr. Makuro. If any of them are shut down permanently, I don't know what I'll do. . . .*

Thresher got a hit on the scope then. It was a small vessel, badly damaged, power completely out. He called up a visual, magnified it a dozen times, and saw that it was one of the Hero craft. He immediately powered up his thrusters and intercepted it.

Linking up the two ships, Thresher moved quickly through the airlocks. Inside, he found Stormer and Stringer, both powered down. At first glance, it didn't look like there was any permanent damage. With some effort, he got them both onto his ship.

Once they were secure, he headed for the asteroid. Hopefully, Bulk and Von Ness would be there. Once the team was whole again, they would deal with whoever had done this.

At least, he hoped they would. He wasn't sure how Mr. Makuro was going to take the updated mission report. This had not, so far, been Hero Factory's finest hour.

Stormer's optic sensors suddenly came back online. He was, to put it mildly, shocked. The last thing he remembered was the freighter exploding and the Hero craft being battered by the shock waves. He was certain that would be the last memory he would ever record. Yet, here he was, in the Hero Factory medical bay. Stringer was already sitting up on a nearby diagnostic bed.

"I was starting to think you were never going to reboot," said Stringer. "You must have been pretty banged up."

"Yeah," said Stormer, sitting up. "What happened? How did we get back here?"

"Thresher saved us. And you're lucky you've been out—it's been a bad few days."

"Days?!" Stormer yelled as he got to his feet. "I've been down for days? What about XT4? How are Bulk and Von Ness? What happened to—?"

"Easy, easy," said Stringer. "Thresher and Zib want us in the briefing room. I guess we'll get all the answers we want there."

When Stringer and Stormer arrived, they saw that Bulk and Von Ness were already there. Bulk stood up and clapped both robots on the back. Von Ness gave a small smile and nodded in their direction. Shortly after all four took their seats, Zib came in, followed by a grim Thresher.

"I'm glad to see you're all in one piece," said the team leader. "We have a lot to go over, so let's not waste time. Zib, turn the screen on."

Zib did as he was told. An image of XT4 appeared on the wall-mounted video screen.

"Is that a picture of your visitor?" Thresher asked. When he saw nods all around, he continued, "That's an XT4 industrial robot, manufactured by Makuhero Industries. A shipment of them was hijacked and apparently destroyed a few days ago. We now believe one of the robots was salvaged and that it was the one who infiltrated Hero Factory."

"I think at this point, Thresher, it might be wise to inform them of the results of the recent . . . misadventures," said Zib.

Thresher looked uncomfortable, but signaled for Zib to keep talking.

"To begin with, the Aird Mining Company is claiming damages to a large number of their mining robots and the subsequent shutdown of an entire mine while replacements were being sent."

"Those miners weren't trying to get stuff out of the ground, they were trying to put me and Stormer in it!" snapped Stringer. "I guess they left that part out, huh?"

"If I may continue," said Zib. "Aird is also upset over the hijacking and later destruction of one of their ore freighters. Fortunately, none of the crew was harmed, but a fortune in valuable ores was lost when the ship blew up . . . an event

Aird believes Hero Factory could have prevented.

"Add to that the enormous damage done to Asteroid J-54, the infiltration of and theft of data from Hero Factory, two Hero craft destroyed and one stolen . . . and you can understand why the galactic media would be spending a great deal of time discussing us these days . . . and not in very flattering terms."

"So we big, bad heroes are scared of a little bad press now?" asked Bulk.

"It's more than just that," said Thresher. "We knew from the start that Hero Factory would only be as good as its reputation. If the galaxy is afraid of us, or doesn't trust us—or worse, thinks we're just blundering around making bad situations worse—then our effectiveness is basically over."

"And we haven't exactly distinguished ourselves lately," said Stormer.

"In more ways than one," added Von Ness.

"That's right," said Thresher. "I wish I didn't have to say this, but . . ."

"I will tell them," offered Zib. "It's the least I can do."

"No, this is my team, and my responsibility," Thresher replied. "I want to say first that it's been an honor to serve with all of you. I know that all of you are true Heroes, through and through. Which just makes it more difficult to tell you that . . . Mr. Makuro has decided to close down Hero Factory."

Stringer, Stormer, and Bulk were on their feet immediately. "What?!" yelled Stringer. "Okay, we screwed up a few times, but—"

"Thresher, you can't let him do this! What about the Legion of Darkness?" cried Stormer.

"The Legion will be dealt with by local law enforcement," Thresher answered, obviously uncomfortable saying the words.

"Come on, Thresher, you don't believe that," Bulk shot back. "Toxic Reapa and the rest of those guys will run rings around any law-bot who tries to take them in. It won't even be a fight."

Only Von Ness remained seated, drumming his fingers on the back of the chair in front of him. "Why don't all of you face facts? Makuro doesn't believe in us. He probably never did. We were just a way for him to test his idea, and we didn't pass the test. So now he'll toss us out with the rest of the used robots and forget we were ever here. Who would want to keep the reminders of a failure around?"

"It's not like that," Thresher insisted. "It's not even that Hero Factory is a bad idea. Maybe it just wasn't the right time."

"Von Ness has a point though," said an agitated Stringer. "What happens to us now?"

Zib took a step forward. "Mr. Makuro has made a very generous offer to hire you as security robots for his various manufacturing plants."

Stringer threw up his hands. Bulk made a noise of disgust and walked away. Von Ness gave a bitter smile and said, "Oh, what an honor. My Hero Core may burst from pride."

"Be quiet," Stormer said to him. Turning to Zib, he said, "What about . . . what about Hero Factory itself?"

"It will be shut down, temporarily," Zib

answered. "Over the coming weeks, it will be retooled to produce robots for deep space exploration."

"I can't believe this," muttered Stormer. "How can it just be . . . over?"

Von Ness got up and headed for the door. "So long. Nice risking my life for nothing with you."

"Wait," Stormer said. "Maybe if we all stick together, we can change Makuro's mind . . . or at least stop the Legion before we go!"

Stringer turned and, not without sympathy, said, "Give it up, kid. Like Thresher said, the Legion is someone else's problem now. Who knows, without us to kick around, they might just fade away."

Stormer turned to the one Hero he thought might stick with him. "Bulk . . . ?"

The big robot shrugged, not even able to bring himself to look at Stormer. "I know it's tough. And I'm pretty sure you would have been the best of us all, Stormer. But I'm not staying someplace I'm not wanted."

At last, Stormer was alone with Thresher. The

leader of Alpha Team kept his distance, letting his friend grieve in private. Then he said, "So what are you going to do, Stormer?"

"I don't know. I can't just give in. I guess I'm not . . . built that way."

"You're not thinking of going after Black Phantom and the others by yourself, are you?"

"Not a good idea?" asked Stormer, doing his best to muster a smile.

"It would be a one-way ticket to the scrap heap," said Thresher, his voice firm. "And you're not doing it. In fact, you're going to stay here and oversee shutdown operations with me. When that's done, we'll decide what comes next."

"I just hope we will be the ones to decide," said Stormer, "and not Black Phantom."

7

At last, the Legion of Darkness, the greatest army of crime ever assembled, was together and ready to strike . . . even if it was in the back room of a refueling station. Black Phantom had his weapons — now he just had to decide how to use them.

There were any number of different ways he could deal a blow to Hero Factory. The Legion could ambush the Heroes one by one, using XT4's knowledge of their strengths and weaknesses to defeat them. Maybe they could even ransom each one back to Makuro . . . that would be a huge humiliation for Hero Factory.

Then again, there was always the spectacular

crime idea. He had at his fingertips some of the top criminals in the galactic underworld, all of them itching for some action. A really huge theft, right under the noses of Hero Factory, would add to the chorus of official voices demanding Makuro explain just what his Heroes were doing and how they were doing it . . . or *not* doing it.

The third option was just to ignore Hero Factory altogether. Pull the crimes they wanted to pull, wherever they wanted to pull them, and if the Heroes showed up, treat them with the contempt they deserve. Defeat them again and again until they learned to stick to small crimes and small criminals and stay out of the Legion's way.

"Hey! Look at this!"

The shout came from Splitface, who had been spending his time since Asteroid J-54 watching news reports on the "daring jailbreak." Most likely, he had just seen one he particularly liked and wanted to share it with the rest of the gang. Needing an excuse to stop plotting and planning, Black Phantom got up to see what was going on.

Splitface was indeed watching the news, but it was a report Black Phantom hadn't expected. "To repeat the latest bulletin," the news anchor said, "Makuhero Industries has announced that Hero Factory will be closed as of the end of this week. No explanation for the decision was given. Critics of the private company's efforts to enforce law and order in the galaxy are hailing Makuro's move as a return to common sense."

"Isn't that a shame, guys?" said Splitface, grinning. "The Heroes have gone out of business. They're packing up and going home."

"That's nothing to be happy about," Toxic Reapa snarled. "I was looking forward to smashing them myself."

"I guess we hit them where it hurt," Jawblade put in. "In Makuro's ego."

Only Speeda Demon seemed wary about the news. He darted from place to place in the room, as if unable to keep still, talking as he ran. "Maybe it's the real thing, or maybe it's a trick. Maybe they just want us to think they're shutting down and actually they'll be waiting to surprise us next time. Yeah, I could see them doing that. Plant a story and then wham, crush us as soon as we show our faces."

XT4 turned to Black Phantom. "There is a 46.7 percent chance that Speeda Demon is correct. I would advise we proceed with caution."

Voltix hurled a lightning bolt, singeing XT4's shoulder armor. "Caution is for fools like Von Ness. We're villains. We don't do caution."

Black Phantom had heard enough. "Okay, quiet down, all of you. I'm not sure what this means any more than you do, but I think Jawblade may be right. I think maybe we embarrassed Makuro enough that he gave up."

Splitface got up and grabbed a can of oil. "So what's this mean for us, boss? We got together to beat Hero Factory, and we beat them. Do we all go solo again, or what?"

Black Phantom smiled. Surprisingly enough, this unexpected news had solved his problem of what to do next. "Quite the opposite, Splitface. With Hero Factory no more, the Legion of Darkness is poised to run this galaxy. But to do that properly, we need a headquarters—not a hideout."

"Let me guess," said Voltix. "You have someplace in mind."

"Oh yes," said Black Phantom. "It's spacious, centrally located, plenty of room for us to design and test new weapons, and it's only had one previous owner. I think Hero Factory HQ will suit the Legion of Darkness just fine."

It was time for good-byes.

Stringer, Bulk, and Von Ness were going to hitch a ride on a Makuhero freighter that would be passing by their new places of employment. Stringer, in particular, insisted this new posting would be temporary. He intended to become a freelance troubleshooter once he had a little more experience. Bulk and Von Ness seemed to be taking the whole thing pretty calmly, with Von Ness insisting he always knew Hero Factory would fail and Bulk pointing out that nothing is forever.

"I'm going to miss you guys," said Stormer. "We did some great things together."

"Not enough, apparently," muttered Von Ness.

"Don't pay attention to this one," Bulk said, shaking Stormer's hand. "We're going to miss you, too, Stormer. When you get done helping Thresher with this place, why not come out and work at one of the plants? Sounds like it's easier than chasing bad robots all day long."

"Maybe I will," said Stormer, unconvincingly. He reached into a pack and produced three small rings of metal. "I made these for you three. They're . . . well, they're Hero Factory signalers. If we're ever, you know, needed, Zib can signal us and we'll get the message wherever we are."

"You never give up hope, do you, Stormer?" Stringer said. But he took the ring anyway. So did the others.

Thresher stuck his head in the room. "You three better get moving. The freighter is ready to get underway."

It was an awkward moment. Promises were

made that messages would be sent once the three ex-Heroes were established in their new roles. For his part, Stormer said he would visit them all and would keep lobbying Mr. Makuro to reestablish Hero Factory.

And then they were gone.

Stormer turned on the console in his quarters and switched it to external camera. The freighter moved slowly away from the planet. He watched it for a long time, his mind on lost friends. He never noticed the two scout ships that hovered just at the edge of sensor range.

Now it was deathly quiet in what had once been Hero Factory.

It wouldn't stay that way for long.

On board one of the scout ships, Speeda Demon studied his scanners. They were covered in little red blips of light, each one representing a security robot in and around Hero Factory or its immediate environs. There were planetary banks that weren't as well-guarded as this facility, he thought.

"Wow," he said to no one in particular. "I thought trying to take over Hero Factory was just kind of a crazy idea. But it's actually a really, really bad idea. I mean catastrophic, we-all-get-plenty-of-time-in-prison-to-regret-this kind of bad."

"Calm down," replied Toxic Reapa. "You need to learn to relax."

Speeda Demon glared at him. "You go around spraying things with toxic sludge. You're not exactly a model of peace and tranquility."

"It will work," said Black Phantom. "Don't forget, we know more about Hero Factory than anyone short of Makuro does. All those red lights? They're about to go out."

On the screen, the second scout ship dropped something that looked like a missile on the outskirts of Makuhero City. "What is that?" asked Speeda Demon. "And aren't they just going to shoot it down?"

"That," said Black Phantom, "is an example of how I do things — no one knows the full plan but me. It's exactly what it looks like, a missile, but it doesn't have any explosive in it. It has Jawblade in it."

"So when they blow it up . . ." began Toxic Reapa.

"They set him free," finished Black Phantom.

Outside, the missile was plummeting toward the city. Automatic laser cannons deployed and blasted it apart in the air. With all the large fragments of the metal shell raining down, no one on the ground noticed Jawblade falling as well. Criminal and shrapnel landed just where they were planned to: in the midst of the Makuhero Reservoir.

Black Phantom nodded. The key to being a good thief was to think in three dimensions. It wasn't just the alarms you could see that you had to worry about, it was the backups, and the backups of the backups. When planning a break-in, you focused on the basic needs the target building and its occupants would have, and then you took advantage of those needs. It was something Jawblade had been doing for years, which is why he had gone along with this part of the plan so easily.

Part of Hero Factory was, in the end, a factory, much like any other. Factories use big machines, and machines need water to keep them cool. Jawblade could get in virtually anywhere water was coming in.

Jawblade was already past the borders of Makuhero City, heading for Hero Factory itself. The channel had moved underground now, but he had memorized XT4's map and knew just where to go. Anything that got in his way—grilles, bars, other physical obstacles—he demolished with his jaws.

XT4 had discovered a flaw in Hero Factory's security. While the Heroes had individual Hero Cores to power them, the robots that guarded the facility did not. They and the weaponry around the place were all powered from the same source, deep inside the factory. Cut off that power, and it would take approximately sixty seconds for the backup system to kick in. The success of the entire plan would depend on what XT4 did in that one minute.

Jawblade took a left branch off the channel, avoiding the certain doom that would have come from proceeding forward, as the water would be boiling up ahead. This branch headed for the central power core. Jawblade knew he didn't have to go that far — there was a three-foot stretch of tunnel where the heavily insulated power lines ran along the ceiling and into the power chamber.

This was crucial. If he missed that spot, he would wind up in the power chamber, taking a radioactive bath he wouldn't swim away from. Again, XT4's information saved the day. Jawblade spotted the thick cables overhead, leapt, and sank his teeth into them. The voltage that coursed through his body was devastatingly powerful and he blacked out, jaws still locked on the wires. But the job was done — the power was cut to the external security systems.

On Black Phantom's scout ship, the red blips on the screen all went out. The leader of the Legion of Darkness shouted into the comm, "Go! Go!"

The two scout ships dove straight for Hero Factory's mission control center.

Inside the Assembly Tower, Stormer saw the lights flicker, then illuminate again. He had never seen anything like that happen here. Checking the wall monitor, he saw that external power was out.

"Stormer to Thresher," he said into his helmet radio. "We have a power outage to the security systems."

"I saw," Thresher replied. "Backup should kick back in, but you better get to the central power core and check it out."

"Right."

Stormer broke into a run. He was almost to the exit when the world caved in.

The two scout ships crashed through the roof of Mission Control, sending metal and masonry raining down to the floor. Once inside, they hovered for a moment, watching for any sign of resistance.

"Let's take this place apart!" growled Splitface.

"We follow the plan," Black Phantom replied, his tone of voice implying that he was not going to take any nonsense. "XT4, go!"

The industrial robot dropped from the other scout ship. He rapidly cleared rubble away from one of the main consoles and plugged himself in. Once inside the system, it would be a simple matter to do his job: close and lock all exterior doors in the complex. Then, when the backup power system kicked in, the security robots would be unable to get inside.

That's what would have happened . . . if Stormer had not slammed into XT4 just at that moment, yanking his arm out of the console port.

"Remember me?" said Stormer as the two crashed to the ground. "You owe me, robot, and I intend to collect!"

"Attacker identified: Hero Stormer," XT4 replied mechanically. "Action: Repel attacker."

XT4 lashed out with two of his arms, staggering Stormer. Stormer ripped loose a power cable and thrust it at his opponent. The electric charge sent XT4 flying across the room.

Above, in the scout ship, Black Phantom was getting a radio message from Speeda Demon. "The sixty seconds have passed. Security robots are beginning to come online and the entrances to the facility are open. What now, Black Phantom? Want us to go down and pound Stormer?"

Black Phantom considered it for a moment and then said, "No. You, Voltix, Thornraxx, and Toxic Reapa hit the Assembly Tower and secure it. Splitface and XT4 can take care of that Hero."

Speeda Demon shot the scout ship back up through the hole in the roof and headed for the Assembly Tower. This time, laser turrets opened fire on the craft along with security robots on the rooftops. Speeda Demon made the ship dive, roll, and do every other trick he knew, but in such close quarters, there was little room to dodge. A couple of good shots sheared through the tail of the ship, giving it all the flying ability of Jawblade after a big meal.

At least there was some good news. There was a bay door open in the Assembly Tower. All Speeda Demon had to do was fly through it and land the ship. He was beginning to think this whole thing might work out after all when the door started to close.

"Ship! Turn ship!" Thornraxx yelled. Being able to fly on his own, Thornraxx had still not adjusted to flying inside of ships and he really didn't like the experience.

"I can't turn!" Speeda Demon snapped back. "It's too narrow here and we're going too fast! So just hang on to something!"

"Turn ship! Turn ship!" Thornraxx shouted again, as the bay door was half-closed now.

"Oh, for . . . come here!" yelled Toxic Reapa. He grabbed Thornraxx by the scruff of the neck, opened the scout ship's hatch, and threw the insectoid out. Everyone on board could hear a nasty splat just before the hatch closed again.

"What did you do that for?" demanded Voltix.

"Ah, he gave me an itch," Toxic Reapa answered as he sat back down. "I was never sure whether to say hi to him or swat him."

"Duck! Duck!" yelled Speeda Demon.

The next instant, the scout ship slammed into the partly closed launch bay door. The thick metal door cut the top off the ship, almost taking Voltix's head off when he didn't get it down quick enough. Then they were inside the Assembly Tower as Speeda Demon struggled to keep the craft in the air.

"Bail out!" he shouted. "This thing is going to crash!"

"By all means, jump," Thresher shouted from below. He was standing atop one of the robot assembly/fusion machines, both his mass driver launchers aimed at the scout ship. "I can hit moving targets just fine."

"Hit this!" replied Voltix, hurling an electric bolt. Thresher leapt aside, falling off the machine and landing on the conveyor belt below. The belt wasn't moving, since the Assembly Tower was powered down. But a little thing like that wasn't going to stop Voltix.

The villain hurled another charge of electricity, this time at the machine, starting it up. The conveyor belt was moving now, carrying Thresher toward a device that would fuse his body together at temperatures hot enough to melt a Hero Core.

Stormer was pinned by Splitface. XT4 was heading his way, laser slicer powering up. The security robots who tried to get in were blasted by the scout ship.

"You were ready to cash it in back in that alley, Stormer." Splitface laughed. "Still willing to go down, figuring your Hero Factory friends will avenge you? Because I don't see any of them around."

"You're one to talk, Splitface," Stormer replied. "Do you really think you can take over Hero Factory and get away with it? Makuhero and every honest planetary government will throw everything they've got at you. All you're doing is making it easier for the law to find you."

"Make this guy keep quiet, XT4," was Splitface's answer.

XT4 closed in, ready to do some spur-of-the-moment "repair" work to Stormer. At the last second, the Hero suddenly pitched forward, hauling Splitface off his feet and putting him between Stormer and XT4. The laser slicer hit Splitface just before Stormer let him go, sending him crashing into his robotic ally.

It was a temporary victory, and Stormer knew it. Black Phantom had his range now, and the scout ship was peppering the floor with rockets. Nor did the Legion of Darkness leader seem to care very much if he hit pretty close to his own allies, as long as he got his target.

XT4 and the now wounded Splitface were already back on their feet. Stormer had to face facts: Without help, he wasn't going to be able to hold Mission Control. Thresher had been working in the Assembly Tower, so he would be busy with the other four Legion members. That left only one hope. But he had to get out of here in one piece first.

Stormer dove for cover, rolled across the floor, and sprang to his feet near a rear door. XT4, Splitface, and the scout ship immediately started blasting, shooting the door off its hinges. They couldn't see Stormer smile. That door led to a top security chamber, and Stormer didn't have access to it yet. But, thanks to Legion weaponry, he did now.

He darted inside and found the inner door. This one was thicker and tougher than the outer door, but the electronic lock was easier to bypass. Stormer got it open just as XT4 and Splitface closed in. He got inside the inner chamber and slammed the door behind him.

This was the Mission Control fail-safe room. Here Zib had installed prototype security systems tied into Mission Control's systems, but they were so dangerous and as yet untested that they were not online. Stormer didn't expect much from them, but if they could buy him a couple of minutes, that would be enough. He had already admitted to himself that he wouldn't be walking away from this fight. He intended to make sure none of the Legion did, either.

Stormer hit the "Activate" button on Zib's jury-rigged security panel. Then he twisted his signal ring, sending out a call for help to the only three robots in the galaxy who could save Hero Factory now.

On board the freighter, Von Ness was the first to notice his signal ring buzzing. "Can you believe it?" he said to Stringer and Bulk. "We just left and Stormer is calling us already."

"Maybe he got lonely," said Stringer. "Or one of the vid screens broke."

"Hey, come on," Bulk said. "What if it's something serious? We might be needed."

Von Ness frowned. "Listen, I'd go back if I

thought something was really wrong. But I think Stormer is just crying Arcturian dragon-wolf here. I'm not going to run back there for nothing."

"Yeah, I suppose you're right." Bulk shrugged. "I mean, he has to still be at Hero Factory. What could possibly menace him there?"

Thresher rolled off the conveyor belt and clung to the frame by his fingers, hanging hundreds of feet above the floor. He could do nothing but watch as Toxic Reapa, Voltix, and Speeda Demon bailed out of the scout ship.

They did so just in time. The badly damaged ship went into a dive, roaring over Thresher's head and smashing into a bank of machinery on the ground before exploding. The blast rocked Thresher, forcing him to let go of his handhold and sending him plummeting toward the flames.

Keeping calm, Thresher aimed and fired his launcher. His missile broke apart into a multiclawed, rotating device that struck a girder and locked in place. It then fired a line back toward Thresher, who grabbed it and swung to safety.

From his new perch atop a massive pipe, he surveyed the scene. The three villains had spread out, but hadn't spotted him yet. As he watched, Speeda Demon took off on a high-speed search of the tower. This left Voltix alone among the stacks of robot parts. Thresher crouched down and ran along the pipe in that direction.

He was almost to his destination when Toxic Reapa spotted him. The villain unleashed a blast of toxic sludge that ate through the pipe Thresher was on. Thresher dove, grabbed another pipe, swung over it, and then did it again farther down. He moved so rapidly that Toxic Reapa couldn't get a good shot and Voltix never saw him coming.

Thresher smashed feetfirst into the electrical villain. Voltix let go of a lightning bolt as he fell, the resulting power surge starting up the Hero assembler/disassembler. A crane arm reached down from above and started snatching up robot pieces from the large bins, then depositing them inside the machine.

With Voltix down, Thresher looked around for insulated wire he could use to tie up the villain. Spotting some, he tore it loose. He was just about to bind Voltix's wrists when Speeda Demon raced by, striking him with a glancing blow. Backed by such tremendous speed, that was enough to send Thresher flying into the wall.

When he had recovered his senses, the Hero was suspended in the air, in the grip of the crane arm. Voltix, Toxic Reapa, and Speeda Demon were down below, looking up at him.

"Nice machines you have here," said Voltix. "That one puts Heroes together . . . or takes them apart. Which do you think it's going to do to you, Thresher?"

Insanity had broken loose in Mission Control. Zib's new security system included a portion of the floor that shot up like a pile driver, which managed to effectively cripple Black Phantom's scout ship. The villain managed to bail out and get to safety right before the wreckage of his vessel crashed to the floor.

XT4, meanwhile, was in battle with a dozen steel tentacles that had sprung from the walls. Individually, none of them were strong enough to hold him, but by attacking as a group, they kept him too off balance to gain any leverage or aim his laser slicer.

That left Splitface alone to pound on the door Stormer was behind. Little by little, the metal was giving before his assault. Finally, with a harsh crack, one of the hinges gave. Smiling wolfishly, Splitface grabbed the edge of the door and pulled, ripping it loose. He threw it aside and charged into the room, to find . . .

Nothing.

Well, not exactly nothing. There was an active monitor screen, but all that was on it was some text. It read, "Surprise, Splitface."

Then the floor fell away and Splitface was

plunging down a metal pipe, going around and around as it spiraled into the bowels of Hero Factory. His yell of rage echoed up from below and then faded.

As soon as he was gone, Stormer dropped down from the ceiling. The next step in his plan called for him to disable Mission Control's main computer systems, then slip away and go help Thresher in the Assembly Tower. It was a good idea, except that Black Phantom wasn't going along with it.

"Stay where you are, Stormer," the leader of the Legion said, his weapon aimed at the young Hero. "You're more resourceful than I gave you credit for. Without my help, XT4 might still be tangled up in those coils. But the race is over, and you've lost."

Stormer raised his hands slowly. Black Phantom never noticed him brushing against a wall switch. "I guess so," said Stormer. "I have to admit, this Legion of Darkness was a good idea. You certainly got what you wanted."

"Not quite yet," answered Black Phantom.

"Splitface and the rest have been useful tools, even if they don't realize it. They actually think I want to turn this dump into our secret headquarters! Imagine, a 'secret' headquarters in a famous building inside a major city—who's dumb enough to think that would work?"

"So . . . you're not out to capture Hero Factory?" asked Stormer, somewhat confused.

"Of course I am."

"But you said . . ."

"Maybe you can learn something, in the little time you have left," Black Phantom said, a sneer in his voice. "I assembled the greatest thieves and smugglers in the galaxy into one team. I used them to eliminate Hero Factory. Then I led them into an indefensible position in your headquarters. As you said before, everyone will be trying to pry us out of here . . . and they'll succeed."

"Then how does any of this make sense?" asked Stormer.

"Let me put this in small words so you can understand it, Hero. The law breaks in here and the whole Legion gets arrested . . . or worse. All except Black Phantom, who mysteriously disappears in the fight. Just like that, I have two things every master thief wants: a reputation, as the criminal who destroyed Hero Factory . . . and no competition."

Stormer couldn't help feeling impressed. This was cunning on a whole new scale. "You set this all up just to get Toxic Reapa and the rest put away, so that you would be the top robot in the underworld."

"And I will be," Black Phantom said, smiling. "I'll publicly vow revenge for what happened to the Legion, but they can rot for all I care. I'll keep XT4 around; he can't help but be loyal. As for the rest . . . what crook won't want to join my *real* gang, since I'm the one who defeated all you Heroes? Now I just have to start tying up loose ends . . . starting with you, Stormer."

"Oh, I wouldn't do that if I were you."

"If you were him, he'd be better looking."

"Could you guys keep quiet and just let me hit something?"

Stormer broke into a grin. He couldn't help it.

Standing behind Black Phantom and XT4 were Bulk, Stringer, and Von Ness.

"You came back!" exclaimed Stormer.

"Turned out Bulk forgot something," said Stringer.

"Yes," agreed Von Ness. "His common sense."

"And look what we found when we got back," Bulk said to Black Phantom. "Mean old you."

Stringer took a step forward. "You're in our house. Do you know what we do to creeps like you in our house?"

"Some wind up on Asteroid J-54," Von Ness said, "the lucky ones, anyway."

"The rest, well, we don't talk about that," said Bulk, with a fierce smile. "We're the good guys, right? We got a reputation to uphold."

"You don't scare me," Black Phantom said, defiantly. "The rest of my Legion is taking the Assembly Tower even now."

"So?" said Bulk. He suddenly reached out and grabbed Black Phantom by the throat, lifting him up in the air. "They got the Tower, and we got you. Assembly Tower's built to take a lot of punishment . . . how about yourself?"

"Wait a minute," said Stormer. "Thresher's in the Tower! He's facing the rest of them alone."

"Warning!" said XT4. "Desist from physical action against leader, or I will retaliate."

"Desist from?" said Stringer. "Who talks like that?"

Before anyone could say anymore, XT4 fired his laser slicer at Bulk, hitting him in the arm. Wounded, he dropped Black Phantom. *"Owwww!"* roared Bulk. "That hurt, you little—"

"Allow me," said Von Ness. "I have a debt to pay."

Taking aim with his gravity weapon, Von Ness fired it at XT4. The effect was immediate as the pull of gravity doubled, tripled, quadrupled around the industrial robot. It was more than the metal floor-ing could handle, which buckled beneath XT4's weight. The next moment, the robot fell through the floor, too heavy to stop himself.

Stringer leaned over and looked down the hole. "I guess it's paid, then. You owed them something?"

"I owed myself," answered Von Ness.

"Hey, where's Black Phantom?" asked Bulk, looking around.

"Must have slipped out," Stormer said. "Probably headed for the Assembly Tower to rally the troops."

"Then just call us rally-killers," said Stringer. "Let's go!"

The four Heroes raced for the entrance to the access tunnel that led to the Assembly Tower. "You know," said Stormer as they ran, "Black Phantom was counting on Hero Factory being finished. You guys showing up just ruined his whole day."

"Probably still is finished," said Bulk. "We're just doing an encore."

In the Assembly Tower, Thresher was still hanging suspended over the disassembly machine, though dropping by inches every minute. The three villains were savoring having the Alpha

Team leader at their mercy, and Thresher had to admit things looked bleak. The crane's claw had his arms pinned so he couldn't use his weapons, and his optic sensors still hadn't fully recovered from Speeda Demon's blow.

Black Phantom suddenly burst into the room. Assessing the situation immediately, he shouted, "What are you idiots doing? Drop him in! Hurry!"

"What's the rush?" asked Toxic Reapa. "I haven't had this much fun in ages."

"The rest of Hero Factory is right behind me, sludge-for-brains. That's the rush!" cried Black Phantom. "If we don't act now, it will be too—"

Part of the wall suddenly flew across the chamber, thanks to the powerful fist of Bulk. Four Heroes stepped into the Assembly Tower, ready for battle.

"Back off!" yelled Voltix. "We've got your leader!"

"You mean you had our leader," Stringer said, using his sonic weapon to sever the crane arm. Von Ness was next, lowering the gravity of both

Thresher and the crane arm until both floated away from the machine. Bulk followed, tearing the claw open and freeing the Alpha Team leader.

"Thanks," said Thresher, getting to his feet. "You guys are back again?"

"Yeah, we hate short good-byes," Stringer replied. "So now what?"

"Even if you do outnumber us, we'll still win," said Black Phantom. "We'll destroy all of Hero Factory, even all of Makuhero City, in the battle. We are the Legion of Darkness!"

"Yeah, about that," said Stormer. He hit a button on the wall. Loudspeakers suddenly boomed to life, broadcasting Black Phantom's voice throughout the Assembly Tower.

"Splitface and the rest have been useful tools, even if they don't realize it. . . . The law breaks in here and the whole Legion gets arrested . . . or worse. . . . I'll publicly vow revenge for what happened to the Legion, but they can rot for all I care. . . ."

Slowly, Toxic Reapa, Voltix, and Speeda Demon turned to look at their leader. "Tools, are we?" said Voltix.

"We can rot, huh?" growled Toxic Reapa.

"Are you going to believe them?" cried Black Phantom. "This is a trick! They want to turn us against each other!"

"Guess what?" said Speeda Demon, menace in his voice. "It worked."

Black Phantom never had time to do what he did best — slip away before things got messy. The combination of a superspeed blow, an electric bolt, and some toxic sludge put him down.

"You know, Stormer, there's one thing we forgot to do when we cleaned this place up," said Thresher, pounding one metal fist into his open hand.

"What's that?"

"Take out the trash," Thresher answered. "So let's do it now."

Speeda Demon calculated some quick odds in his head. The remnants of the Legion were outnumbered and on Hero Factory's turf. Coming here had been a bad idea to start with, and staying here was an even worse one.

"I'm gone," he said, already kicking in his superspeed and racing for the exit.

"Don't be in such a hurry," said Von Ness. Using his gravity weapon, he made Speeda Demon feel like he was running through a swamp. Try as he might, he couldn't get any speed up.

"Maybe he's scared to face you, but we're not," snarled Toxic Reapa. "Come on, Voltix, you sizzle 'em and I'll sludge 'em."

Stormer unleashed two explosive bursts from his weapon in rapid succession, knocking both villains off their feet. "I've got a better idea. I'll smash you — "

"And I'll smash you some more," said Bulk, hauling both villains to their feet before clanging their heads together.

"That's a heck of a sound they just made," said Stringer. "Must be because both their heads are hollow. Let me see if I can duplicate it."

Bulk let go of the two dazed Legion members

and stepped aside. Stringer adjusted his sonic blaster and hit them with a wave of concentrated sound that vibrated every circuit in their robot bodies. Overwhelmed, they both collapsed to the floor.

Meanwhile, Speeda Demon was still trying to escape. He didn't care if, with the increased gravity, it would now take him a full day to make it to the exit—he wasn't staying here and fighting five Heroes by himself.

Then he felt a tap on his shoulder.

It took a while for Speeda Demon to turn his head, thanks to Von Ness's games with gravity. When he finally did, he saw an angry Thresher.

"Where do you think you're going?" said the Alpha Team leader.

"Um . . . back to prison?"

"Good guess," said Thresher. "Your life is about to slow way down, SD."

It had been three days since the defeat of the Legion of Darkness. Clean-up operations had included getting Jawblade out of the water system, retrieving Splitface from the sub-basement, and patching up Thornraxx before shipping him and the others to Asteroid J-54. There was still a lot of damage to Mission Control and the Assembly Tower that would have to be repaired, but Zib believed it could all be fixed relatively quickly.

Stormer couldn't help but feel good. Hero Factory had survived its toughest test, jailed several dangerous criminals, and shown the galaxy what it could do. As soon as the news of this victory spread, each and every world would be demanding the help of the Heroes.

He walked into Mission Control to find Thresher recording the last of the log entry on the case. Then he saw him file it as "Classified, Security Protocol 1-A."

"Top security?" asked Stormer. "Doesn't really make sense, does it, when this story is sure to be all over the news?"

"No, it won't," said Thresher. "No one is ever going to hear about this."

"What? Why? This was a great victory!"

"It was almost a horrible defeat," said Thresher. "We were lucky. If you hadn't made those signal rings, if Bulk and the others hadn't come back . . . who knows what would have happened? Hero Factory and all its secrets could have been in the hands of Black Phantom."

"But they're not," argued Stormer. "We stood together and we beat him!"

Thresher stood up. "Listen to me. Innocents could have been hurt. This whole place could have been destroyed. I'm not going to give any other would-be criminal masterminds the idea that all they need to do is form a team and hit Makuhero City. This file stays closed. Got it?"

Stormer wanted to argue some more, but he could see from the look on Thresher's face that it would do no good. "What about the Legion members?"

"Even if they get out of prison someday—which I doubt—I can't see them ever working together again," said Thresher. "They hate each other. Hopefully, we'll just be dealing with them one at a time from now on."

"Okay. Where are Stringer and the others?"

"Upstairs. Zib called a briefing session. Then they're scheduled to get on another freighter and head for their new posts."

Stormer felt like someone had punched him. "You mean . . . Hero Factory is still shutting down?"

"I haven't heard anything different," Thresher replied. "Let's go."

Zib and the rest were already there when Thresher and Stormer arrived. The Heroes were surprised to see their leader sitting down with them, as opposed to running the meeting. Apparently, this one was Zib's show.

"I just wanted to convey Mr. Makuro's congratulations on your victory," began Zib. "It takes a special kind of courage to keep fighting even when everyone wants you to quit."

Nobody knew what to say to that, so they kept quiet.

"Mr. Makuro says he wishes to have that same

kind of courage," Zib continued. "Many people think he should shut down Hero Factory and use his wealth to do something simpler and safer. But while he was playing it safe, everyone else in the known universe would be in greater danger . . . with no Heroes to protect them."

Zib took a deep breath and exhaled with a smile. "That is why he has decided, as of now, to reopen Hero Factory. We're back in business!"

The room rocked with cheers from the assembled Heroes. Only Von Ness seemed less than excited about the news.

Later that day, Mr. Makuro would appear on vidscreens throughout known space. "In years to come," he said, "many other Heroes will be created in the Assembly Tower and go out into the universe to fight for justice. They will have different names and different powers from the members of this first team, but they will share the commitment to peace and safety for every living being.

"Each Hero who walks these halls will have the courage, the sense of honor, and the willingness to risk all to save others. Today, I give you my word that Hero Factory will always be here to serve and protect the innocent and to punish the guilty."

And so it has been, from that time to this. . . .

Epilogue

urno clicked off the monitor. "That was some story."

"Yeah, we almost didn't walk away from that one," said Bulk. "Too bad we didn't know at the time that Von Ness had let Voltix and Toxic Reapa get away. Might have saved us a lot of trouble down the line."

Furno nodded. "I can guess how much it must have hurt Stormer when Von Ness deserted Hero Factory and later reappeared as the villain Von Nebula."

"Hurt all of us," Bulk said. "There he helped us stop Black Phantom and the rest, and he wound up just as bad as any of them."

"Given all that happened, I'm surprised that they all broke out of jail together this time around," said Furno.

Stormer's voice came from behind them. "They broke out . . . just not together."

Bulk turned around. "How long have you been standing there?"

"Long enough."

"You going to put me on pipe-cleaning duty for this?" asked Bulk. "It's been a lot of years, Stormer. I figured the rookie had the right to know the truth, tough spots and all."

Stormer shook his head. "Maybe you're right. One of these days, Furno might be doing my job, and he might face just as big a challenge as we did back then. He might as well see how it was done in the old days."

"We *were* a little rough around the edges." Bulk smiled. "Not to mention we were murder on the Hero craft."

"What happened to Thresher?" asked Furno.

"Retired," said Stormer. "Or as much as someone like him can retire. He's head of security on a planet so covert its name doesn't even appear on star charts. They do very secret work there, something to do with defense against mind powers. He says it's not as exciting as it sounds, but at least his headquarters hasn't been wrecked yet."

"Another question—did anything change after this whole Legion of Darkness invasion? Or did things pretty much stay the same?"

"A lot changed," said Bulk.

"All the external security runs on independent power sources now, so what Jawblade did couldn't be done again," said Stormer. "The buildings are ringed with defense screens so nobody can come crashing through our ceiling. Of course, the biggest change is that right after this adventure, Hero Factory started turning out Heroes and making new teams. That's why we're as big as we are now."

"What about Zib's security systems? It sure seemed like they saved the day."

Bulk winced. "Oh, kid, don't ever ask Zib about those. Not something he wants to remember."

"Why not?"

"Well, see . . . you tell it, Stormer. You were there."

"So were you, and closer, as I recall."

"Okay, well, after that fight was over, Stormer here kind of forgot to turn off Zib's systems. Nobody noticed, until Mr. Makuro flew over on his shuttle to inspect the damage to Mission Control. As soon as he flew down through the hole in the roof, the pile driver sort of . . . well . . . crushed his ship."

"Oh no," said Furno, starting to laugh.

"Makuro wasn't hurt," Stormer said, "but it wasn't the most comfortable moment I ever had here . . . or Zib, for that matter. So the systems got officially 'retired' that day."

"You're right, Bulk, a lot has changed," said Furno.

"And some things haven't," said Stormer, his tone turning grim. "We still have escaped criminals out there. The breakout is the worst thing to happen to Hero Factory since the Legion of Darkness, the biggest threat to the public's faith in us. We need to bring all the escapees back, and fast."

Furno pushed his chair away from the desk and stood up. "In other words, enough worrying about yesterday . . ."

Stormer turned and walked out, saying as he went, "Let's go fix tomorrow."